Little House
Parties

THE LITTLE HOUSE
CHAPTER BOOKS
Adapted from the Little House books
by Laura Ingalls Wilder
Illustrated by Renée Graef

A LITTLE HOUSE CHAPTER BOOK

LITTLE HOUSE
The Laura Years

Little House Parties

Adapted from the Little House books by

LAURA   INGALLS   WILDER

illustrated by

RENÉE   GRAEF

HarperCollins*Publishers*

Adaptation by Heather Henson.

*Illustrations for this book are inspired by the work of Garth Williams
with his permission, which we gratefully acknowledge.*

HarperCollins®, 🏠®, Little House®, and The Laura Years™
are trademarks of HarperCollins Publishers Inc.

Little House Parties
Text adapted from *Little House in the Big Woods*, text copyright 1932,
copyright renewed 1959, Roger Lea MacBride; *On the Banks of Plum Creek*,
text copyright 1937, copyright renewed 1965, Roger Lea MacBride;
Little Town on the Prairie, text copyright 1941, copyright renewed
1969, Roger Lea MacBride.
Illustrations copyright © 1999 by Renée Graef
For information address HarperCollins
Children's Books, a division of HarperCollins Publishers,
10 East 53rd Street, New York, NY 10022.
http://www.harperchildrens.com

Library of Congress Cataloging-in-Publication Data
Little house parties : [adapted from the Little house books by Laura Ingalls
Wilder] / illustrated by Renée Graef.
    p.   cm. — (A Little house chapter book)
Summary: From the maple syrup party at her grandpa's house in the Big
Woods in Wisconsin to parties with her school friends in Plum Creek and her
first co-ed party in De Smet, Dakota Territory, Laura enjoys all kinds of
gatherings.
    ISBN 0-06-027951-6 (lib. bdg.). — ISBN 0-06-442085-X (pbk.)
    1. Wilder, Laura Ingalls, 1867–1957—Juvenile fiction.   [1. Wilder,
Laura Ingalls, 1867–1957—Fiction.   2. Frontier and pioneer life—Fiction.
3. Parties—Fiction.]   I. Wilder, Laura Ingalls, 1867–1957.   II. Graef, Renée,
ill.   III. Series.
PZ7.L73463   1999   98-41707
[Fic]—dc21   CIP
                                                                 AC

2   3   4   5   6   7   8   9   10
❖
First Edition, 1999

Contents

CHAPTER 1

Going to Grandpa's

Winter was almost over in the Big Woods of Wisconsin where Laura lived with her Ma, her Pa, her big sister Mary, and her little sister Carrie. For days the sun shone and the weather was warm. The icicles dropped one by one from the roof of their little log cabin. The trees shook their wet branches, and chunks of snow fell.

Pa had been helping Grandpa collect sap from the trees in the Big Woods. Grandpa and Pa boiled the sap in a big kettle to make maple syrup.

1

One night, Pa came home late from helping Grandpa. He sat down in front of the fire and took Laura and Mary on his knees. He told them that Grandpa was almost finished making maple syrup.

"He's going to finish up next Monday," Pa said. "He says we must all come to his house to celebrate."

Pa's blue eyes twinkled. He had been saving the best for last.

"Hey, Caroline," he said to Ma, "there'll be a dance!"

Ma smiled. She looked very happy. She laid down her mending for a minute.

"Oh, Charles," she said.

Then she went on with her mending, but she kept on smiling. "I'll wear my delaine dress," she said.

Ma's delaine dress was beautiful. It was dark green, with a little pattern all over it that looked like strawberries. A dressmaker had made it in the East. That's where Ma had come from before she married Pa and moved out west to the Big Woods of Wisconsin.

The dress was kept wrapped in paper and laid away. Laura and Mary had never seen Ma wear it. But she had shown it to them once. She had let them touch the beautiful dark red buttons that buttoned up the front. She had shown them how tiny and perfect the stitches were.

The dance must be very important if Ma was going to wear the beautiful delaine dress. Laura and Mary were excited. They bounced up and down on Pa's knee and asked questions about the dance.

Finally, Pa said with a laugh, "Now you girls run along to bed! You'll know all about the dance when you see it."

Laura couldn't wait until Monday.

When Monday morning finally arrived, everybody in the little house got up early. They were all in a hurry to get to Grandpa's. Pa wanted to be there to help gather and boil the sap. Ma would help Grandma and the aunts make good things to eat for all the people who were coming to the dance.

They ate breakfast and did the morning chores quickly. Pa packed his fiddle carefully in its box and then pulled the big sled up to the gate.

Outside, the air was cold and frosty. Pa tucked them all under blankets in the sled, and away they went.

The horses shook their heads and pranced. The sleigh bells rang merrily as the sled rushed through the Big Woods to

 4

Grandpa's house. Laura felt snug and warm under the layers of robes.

In no time at all they came to Grandpa's house. Grandma came to the door and stood there smiling, calling to them to come in.

Grandma said that Grandpa and Uncle George were already working in the maple woods. So Pa went to help them. Laura and Mary and Ma, with Baby Carrie in her arms, went into Grandma's house and took off their wraps.

Laura loved Grandma's house. It was much larger than their house at home. There was one great big room. Then there was a little room that belonged to Uncle George. And there was another room for the aunts, Aunt Docia and Aunt Ruby. And then there was the kitchen, with a big cookstove.

The day seemed very short. Laura and Mary played while Ma helped Grandma and the aunts in the kitchen. Laura liked to run the whole length of the big room. The floor was made of wide, thick slabs of wood. It was smoothed all over, and scrubbed clean and white.

The whole house smelled good. There were the sweet, spicy smells from the kitchen. There was the smell of the logs burning in the fireplace. And there was the smell of a clove-apple on the table in the big room.

At suppertime Pa and Grandpa and Uncle George came back from the woods with buckets full of hot maple syrup. Grandma put a huge brass kettle on the stove, and Pa and Grandpa poured the syrup into it.

Uncle George was home from the

army. He wore his blue army coat with the brass buttons and he had bold, merry blue eyes. He was big and broad.

Laura looked at him all the time she was eating supper. She had heard Pa say to Ma that he was a wild man. Laura had never seen a wild man before. She did not know whether she was afraid of Uncle George or not.

When supper was over, Uncle George went outside the door and blew his army bugle. It made a lovely, ringing sound, far away through the Big Woods. The woods were dark and silent, and the trees stood still as though they were listening.

Laura went outside to watch Uncle George play his bugle. But when he stopped, she ran quickly back into the house.

Ma and Grandma were tidying up the

kitchen while Aunt Docia and Aunt Ruby made themselves pretty in their room.

Laura sat on the aunts' bed and watched them comb out their long hair. They brushed it so smooth, it shone like silk in the lamplight. They parted it carefully and braided it into long braids. Then they coiled their long braids into big knots behind their heads.

When they were finished with their hair, they pulled on their beautiful white stockings. The aunts had knitted the stockings themselves with fine cotton thread. Over the stockings, they buttoned up their best shoes.

Laura watched them as they helped each other with their corsets. The corsets made their waists smaller. Then Aunt Ruby and Aunt Docia put on their flannel petticoats and their plain petticoats and

their stiff white petticoats. Finally, they put on their beautiful dresses.

The aunts looked lovely. They sailed over the floor so smoothly with their large, round skirts. Their cheeks were a pretty pink and their eyes were bright under the wings of shining, sleek hair.

Ma was beautiful, too. She was wearing her dark green delaine dress. The little leaves on it looked like strawberries. The skirt was ruffled, and it was trimmed with knots of dark green ribbon. Nestled at Ma's throat was a sparkling gold pin. Ma looked so rich and fine that Laura was afraid to touch her.

People began to arrive at Grandpa's house. Some came on foot through the snowy woods. Their lanterns danced in the dark. Others drove up to the door in sleds and in wagons. Sleigh bells jangled all the time.

Laura could hardly be still. She was so excited to see her very first dance.

CHAPTER 2

Dance at Grandpa's

Grandpa and Grandma's big room soon filled with tall boots and swishing skirts and laughing voices. Laura had never seen so many people in one room before.

Uncle George was blowing his bugle. It made a loud, ringing sound in the big room. He joked and laughed and danced, blowing his bugle.

Then Pa took his fiddle out of its box and began to play. All the couples stood in squares on the floor and began to dance when Pa called out.

"Grand right and left!" Pa cried.

Laura watched as all the skirts began to swirl and all the boots began to stamp. The circles went round and round. The skirts went one way and the boots went another. When they came together, all the hands clasped high up in the air.

"Swing your partners!" Pa called.

All the skirts and boots did exactly as Pa said.

Laura could see Ma in among the other dancers. Ma's skirt was swaying, and her dark head was bowing. Laura thought Ma was the loveliest dancer in the world. And Pa's fiddle was singing a bright, happy tune:

> *"Oh, you Buffalo gals,*
> *Aren't you coming out tonight,*
> *Aren't you coming out tonight,*
> *Aren't you coming out tonight,*

 12

Oh, you Buffalo gals,
Aren't you coming out tonight,
To dance by the light of the moon?"

The little circles and the big circles went round and round. The skirts swirled, and the boots stamped. The partners bowed to one another and danced away, and then bowed again.

Laura could not keep her feet still. Uncle George looked at her and laughed. Then he caught her by the hand and did a little dance with her. Laura decided she liked Uncle George.

In the kitchen, Grandma was all by herself. She was stirring the boiling syrup in the big brass kettle. She stirred in time to the music. But soon, everybody was laughing by the kitchen door. They were dragging Grandma into the big room.

Grandma's dress was beautiful, too. It was dark blue calico with leaves scattered over it. Her cheeks were pink from laughing, and she was shaking her head. The wooden spoon was in her hand.

"I can't leave the syrup," she cried.

Pa began to play a fast tune. Everybody began to clap in time to the music. Grandma bowed to them all and did a few

 14

steps by herself. She could dance as prettily as any of them.

Suddenly, Uncle George stepped up and bowed low before Grandma. He began to jig along to the music.

Grandma tossed her spoon to somebody. She put her hands on her hips and faced Uncle George. Everybody shouted. Grandma was jigging.

Laura clapped her hands in time to the music. Grandma's eyes were snapping, and her cheeks were red. Underneath her skirts, her heels were clicking as fast as the thumping of Uncle George's boots.

Everybody was excited. Uncle George kept on jigging. Grandma kept on facing him and jigging, too.

The fiddle did not stop. Uncle George began to breathe loudly. He wiped the sweat off his forehead.

Grandma's eyes twinkled.

"You can't beat her, George!" some-body shouted.

Uncle George jigged faster. He jigged twice as fast as he had been jigging. So did Grandma. Everybody cheered again. All the women were laughing and clapping their hands. All the men were teasing George.

Pa's blue eyes were snapping as he played. He was standing up, watching George and Grandma. The bow danced over the fiddle strings. Laura jumped up and down and clapped her hands.

Grandma kept on jigging. Her hands were on her hips and her chin was up. She was smiling.

George kept on jigging, but his boots did not thump as loudly as they had thumped at first. Grandma's heels kept on clickety-clacking.

 16

All at once, George threw up both arms. "I'm beat!" he gasped and stopped jigging.

Everybody made a big noise, shouting and yelling and stamping. They all cheered Grandma.

Grandma jigged just a little minute more, then she stopped. She laughed in gasps. Her eyes sparkled just like Pa's when she laughed. George was laughing, too.

Suddenly Grandma stopped laughing. She turned and ran into the kitchen. The fiddle had stopped playing. Everyone stood still, waiting.

Grandma came back to the door and smiled. "The syrup is waxing," she said. "Come and help yourselves."

Everybody began to talk and laugh again. They all hurried to the kitchen for plates. Then they went outside to fill their plates with snow. The kitchen door was open, and the cold air came rushing in.

Outside, the stars were frosty in the sky. Laura's breath was like smoke.

She and the other children scooped up clean snow with their plates. Then they went back into the crowded kitchen.

Grandma stood by the brass kettle. With the big wooden spoon, she poured hot syrup on each plate of snow. It cooled into soft candy. As fast as it cooled they ate it.

The children ate the maple candy until they could eat no more. Then they helped themselves to pumpkin pies and dried berry pies and cookies and cakes. There was bread and cold pork and pickles, too. Oo, how sour the pickles were!

After they had eaten as much as they could hold, they began to dance again.

The big room was loud and merry. The

fiddle played and everyone danced.

Grandma stayed in the kitchen, stirring the syrup. Finally, it was ready.

"It's graining!" Grandma called.

Aunt Ruby and Aunt Docia and Ma left the dance and ran into the kitchen. They set out big pans and small pans. As fast as Grandma filled them with the syrup, they set out more. They set the filled ones away, to cool into maple sugar.

The fiddling and the dancing went on and on. All the beautiful skirts went swirling by. All the boots went stamping. The fiddle kept on singing.

Laura had never had so much fun before. The dancing was so pretty and the music so gay, she knew she could never get tired of it.

CHAPTER 3

Town Party

Soon after the dance at Grandpa's, Laura and her family left the Big Woods of Wisconsin. Pa moved them first to the Kansas prairie, and then to a new little farm in Minnesota.

The farm was near a creek called Plum Creek. It was only two and a half miles from town. That meant that Laura and Mary could go to school.

At first Laura didn't want to go to school. She didn't want to meet new people. And she didn't want to leave Ma and Pa and Carrie and her good old bulldog, Jack, every morning.

But soon, Laura realized she liked school after all. She was learning new things and making new friends.

Laura's special friend was a girl named Christy Kennedy. Christy had dark blue eyes and bright red hair in stiff braids down her back.

Laura liked all the girls at school except for one—Nellie Oleson. Nellie was very pretty, but she wasn't very nice. She had yellow hair that hung in long curls. She always wore pretty store-bought dresses because her father owned the store in town.

When Nellie had first seen Laura, she had wrinkled up her nose and called her a country girl. Laura *was* a country girl, and she was proud of it. But Nellie had said it as if Laura should be ashamed.

One day, Nellie invited all the girls at school to a party at her house. Besides the dance at Grandpa's, Laura and Mary had never been to a party. They wondered what it would be like. Ma said it would be a pleasant time to spend with friends.

After school on Friday, Ma washed Laura's and Mary's dresses and sunbonnets. On Saturday morning, she ironed them, fresh and crisp. Laura and Mary bathed that morning, too.

"You look sweet and pretty as posies," Ma said when they came down the ladder. She tied on their hair ribbons and warned them not to lose them.

"Now be good girls," she said, "and mind your manners."

When they came to town, they stopped for Christy and her older sister, Cassie. Christy and Cassie had never been to a party, either. They all went timidly into Mr. Oleson's store.

"Go right in!" Mr. Oleson told them.

So they went past the candy and pickles and plows, to the back of the store. The door opened, and there stood Nellie, all dressed up. Mrs. Oleson stood beside her and asked them to come in.

Laura had never seen such a fine room. The whole floor was covered with some kind of heavy cloth that felt rough under Laura's bare feet. It was brown and green and red and yellow.

The walls and the ceiling were made from narrow, smooth boards. The table and chairs were made from a yellow wood that shone like glass. There were colored pictures on the walls.

Laura wanted to be still and just look at everything, but Mrs. Oleson said,

"Now, Nellie, bring out your playthings."

"They can play with Willie's playthings," Nellie said.

Willie was Nellie's little brother. He was just as mean as his sister. "They can't ride my velocipede!" Willie shouted.

"Well, they can play with your Noah's ark and your soldiers," said Nellie, and Mrs. Oleson made Willie be quiet.

The Noah's ark was the most wonderful thing that Laura had ever seen. They all knelt down and squealed and laughed over it. There were all kinds of animals, just as if the picture had come out of the paper-covered Bible at home.

There were zebras and elephants and tigers and horses.

And there were two whole armies of tin soldiers, with uniforms painted bright blue and bright red.

There was a jumping-jack. He was cut out of thin, flat wood. He had on striped paper trousers and jacket. His face was painted white with red cheeks and circles around his eyes. His tall cap was pointed. He hung between two thin red strips of wood. When you squeezed the pieces of wood, he danced.

Even Mary and the other big girls were squealing over the animals and the soldiers. They laughed at the jumping-jack till they cried.

Then Nellie walked among them, saying, "You can look at my doll."

The doll had a china head, with smooth red cheeks and a red mouth. Her eyes were black, and her china hair was black and waved. Her hands were china, and she had tiny china feet in black china shoes.

"Oh!" Laura said. "Oh, what a beautiful

doll! Oh, Nellie, what is her name?"

"She's nothing but an old doll," Nellie said. "I don't care about this old doll. You wait till you see my new doll."

She threw the china doll in a drawer, and she took out a long box. She put the box on the bed and took off its lid. All the girls leaned around her to look.

There lay a doll that seemed to be alive. Real golden hair lay in soft curls on her little pillow. Her lips were parted, showing two tiny white teeth. Her eyes were closed. The doll was sleeping there in the box.

Nellie lifted her up, and her eyes opened wide. They were big blue eyes. She seemed to laugh. Her arms stretched out and she said, "Mamma!"

"She does that when I squeeze her stomach," Nellie said. "Look!"

Nellie punched the doll's stomach hard with her fist, and the doll cried out, "Mamma!"

The doll was dressed in blue silk. Her petticoats were real petticoats trimmed with the ruffles and lace. On her feet were real little blue leather slippers.

All this time Laura had not said a word. She couldn't. She did not think of actually touching that doll. But without meaning to, her finger reached out toward the blue silk.

"Don't you touch her!" Nellie screeched. "You keep your hands off my doll, Laura Ingalls!"

Nellie snatched the doll against her. She turned her back so Laura could not see her putting the doll back in the box.

Laura's face burned hot, and the other girls did not know what to do. Laura went and sat on a chair. The others watched Nellie put the box in a drawer and shut it. Then they looked at the animals and the soldiers again and squeezed the jumping-jack.

Mrs. Oleson came in and asked Laura why she was not playing.

"I would rather sit here, thank you, ma'am," Laura answered politely.

"Would you like to look at these?" Mrs. Oleson asked her, and she laid two books in Laura's lap.

"Thank you, ma'am," Laura said.

She turned the pages of the books carefully. Laura had not known there were such wonderful books in the world. Laura could read some of them. She soon forgot all about the party.

Suddenly, Mrs. Oleson was saying, "Come little girl. You mustn't let the others eat all the cake, must you?"

"Yes, ma'am," Laura said. "No, ma'am."

There was a beautiful sugar-white cake sitting on the table with tall glasses around it.

"I got the biggest piece," Nellie shouted, grabbing a big piece out of the cake with her fingers. The others sat waiting till Mrs. Oleson gave them their pieces. She put each piece on a china plate.

"Is your lemonade sweet enough?" Mrs. Oleson asked. So Laura knew that it was lemonade in the glasses. She had never tasted anything like it. At first it was sweet. But after she ate a bit of cake, the lemonade was sour. But they all answered Mrs. Oleson politely, "Yes, thank you, ma'am."

They were careful not to let a crumb

of that cake fall on the tablecloth. They did not spill one drop of lemonade.

Then it was time to go home. Laura and Mary remembered to say, "Thank you, Mrs. Oleson. I had a very good time at the party," just as Ma had told them to. So did all the other girls.

When they were out of the store, Christy said to Laura, "I wish you'd slapped that mean Nellie Oleson."

"Oh no! I couldn't!" Laura whispered. "But I'm going to get even with her. Shh! Don't let Mary know I said that."

When they got home, they told Ma about the party.

She said, "We must not accept hospitality without making some in return. I've been thinking about it, girls. You must ask Nellie Oleson and the others to a party here. I think a week from Saturday."

CHAPTER 4

Country Party

"Will you come to my party?" Laura asked Christy and Maud and Nellie. Mary asked the big girls. They all said they would come.

That Saturday morning the house was specially pretty. Jack could not come in. The windows were shining, and the pink-edged curtains were crisp and white.

And Ma made vanity cakes. She made them with beaten eggs and white flour. She dropped them into a kettle of sizzling fat. Each one came up bobbing. Then it floated till it turned itself over, lifting up

32

its honey brown, puffy bottom. When it was round and swollen underneath, Ma lifted it out with a fork.

She would not let Laura and Mary taste any of the little cakes. She put every one of them in the cupboard. They were for the party.

Laura and Mary and Ma and Carrie were dressed up and waiting when the guests came walking out from town.

Laura had even brushed Jack. He was clean and handsome in his white and brown-spotted fur. He ran down with Laura to the creek.

The girls came laughing and splashing through the sunny water. All except for Nellie. She was wearing a new dress and big, new bows in her hair.

She had taken off her shoes and stockings, and she complained that the gravel hurt her feet.

"I don't go barefoot," she said as if going barefoot was shameful.

"Is that Jack?" Christy asked. They all patted him and said what a good dog he was. But when he politely wagged to Nellie, she said, "Go away! Don't you touch my dress!"

The girls walked up the path between the blowing grasses and wildflowers. At the house, Ma was waiting. Mary told her the girls' names one by one. Ma smiled her lovely smile and spoke to them.

But Nellie smoothed down her new pretty dress and said to Ma, "Of course I didn't wear my best dress to just a country party."

Then Laura didn't care what Ma had taught her. She didn't care if Pa punished her. She was going to get even with Nellie for that. Nellie couldn't speak that way to Ma.

Ma only smiled and said, "It's a very pretty dress, Nellie. We're glad you could come."

But Laura was not going to forgive Nellie.

The girls liked the pretty house. It was so clean and airy, with breezes blowing through it and the grassy prairies all around. They climbed the ladder and looked at Laura's and Mary's very own attic. None of them had anything like that.

But Nellie only asked, "Where are your dolls?"

Laura had a rag doll named Charlotte. But she was not going to show her darling Charlotte to Nellie Oleson.

"I don't play with dolls," Laura said. "I play in the creek."

Then they went outdoors with Jack. They ran down the hill to the low bank of Plum Creek and looked at the sparkling pebbles and gurgling water.

Mary and the big girls came down slowly, bringing Carrie to play with. They took Carrie wading where the water sparkled thin in the sunshine. Laura and Christy and Maud and Nellie played tag. They ran on the warm grass, and played in the water.

And while they were playing, Laura suddenly thought of what she could do to Nellie.

An old crab lived under a rock near the water's edge. Laura led the girls wading near the old crab's home. The noise and splashing had driven him under his rock. Laura could see his angry claws and head peeping out, and she crowded Nellie near

 36

him. Then she kicked a big splash of water onto his rock and she screamed, "Oo, Nellie! Nellie, look out!"

The old crab rushed at Nellie's toes, snapping his claws at them.

"Run! Run!" Laura screamed. She pushed Christy and Maud back toward the bridge and ran after Nellie.

Nellie ran screaming straight into the muddy water under the plum thicket. Laura stopped on the gravel and looked back at the crab's rock.

"Wait, Nellie," Laura said. "Stay there."

"Oh, what was it? What was it?" Nellie asked.

"It's an old crab," Laura told her. "He cuts big sticks in two with his claws. He could cut our toes right off."

"Oh, where is he? Is he coming?" Nellie asked.

"You stay there, and I'll look," said Laura, and she went wading slowly and stopping and looking. The old crab was under his rock again, but Laura did not say so. She waded very slowly all the way to the bridge, while Nellie watched from the plum thicket. Then she waded back and said, "You can come out now."

Nellie came out into the clean water. She said she wasn't going to play in that horrid old creek anymore. She tried to wash her muddy skirt and her feet, and then she screamed.

Something was stuck to her. All over her legs and feet were small brown worms the color of mud.

Once Laura had wandered into that same muddy water, and the same worms had stuck to her legs. She had yelled and yelled. When she tried to pull the worms off, they stretched out long and thin until they popped off. It had made her feel sick. Pa said the worms were called bloodsuckers. Ma said they were leeches, and doctors used them to heal sick people.

Nellie tried to pick a leech off, and then she ran screaming up on the creek bank. There she stood, kicking as hard as she could, first one foot and then the other, screaming all the time.

Laura laughed till she fell on the grass and rolled.

"Oh, look, look!" she shouted, laughing. "See Nellie dance!"

All the girls came running. Mary told Laura to pick those bloodsuckers off Nellie, but Laura didn't listen. She kept rolling and laughing.

"Laura!" Mary said. "You get up and

pull those things off, or I'll tell Ma."

Then Laura began to pull the blood-suckers off Nellie. All the girls watched and screamed while she pulled them out long and longer until they popped off.

"I don't like your party!" Nellie cried. "I want to go home!"

Ma came hurrying down to the creek to see why they were screaming. She told Nellie not to cry, a few leeches were nothing to cry about. She said it was time now for them all to come to the house.

The table was set prettily, with Ma's best white cloth and the blue pitcher full of flowers. Shiny tin cups were full of cold, creamy milk. The big platter was heaped with honey-colored vanity cakes.

The cakes were not sweet, but they were rich and crisp, and hollow inside. The crisp bits of it melted on the tongue.

The girls ate and ate those vanity cakes. They said they had never tasted anything so good, and they asked Ma what they were.

"Vanity cakes," said Ma. "Because they are all puffed up, like vanity, with nothing solid inside."

There were so many vanity cakes that they ate till they could eat no more. They drank all the milk they could hold.

Then the party was over. All the girls said thank you for the party except Nellie. Nellie was still mad.

Laura did not care. She thought of Nellie dancing on the creek bank. Deep down inside her, she smiled.

CHAPTER 5

A New Hairstyle

A few short years later, things had changed for Laura. She was no longer a little country girl. She was a big girl, and she lived in town.

Pa had moved farther west, to the town of De Smet in Dakota Territory. During the summer, the family lived on their prairie farm. But during the long, hard winters, the family lived in town.

Laura was going to a new school in town, and now Carrie was old enough to go with her. And there was a new baby in the family named Grace.

Mary was far away at a school in Iowa. She had caught scarlet fever in Plum Creek, and the illness had left her blind. Ma and Pa had heard that there were schools for the blind, so they had saved up their money to send her to one.

Every morning, Laura and Carrie walked down the main street of the little town to school. Laura liked school. She had many friends. There was Mary Power and Ida Brown and Minnie Johnson. And there was Cap Garland and Ben Woodworth and Arthur Johnson, too.

With so many friends, Laura had almost forgotten about Nellie Oleson back in Plum Creek. Then one day, Nellie came to Laura's school! Mr. Oleson had moved west, too. But now he was a farmer instead of a storekeeper, so Nellie was a country girl.

Nellie was even prettier than she had been when Laura knew her in Minnesota. But she was still mean. She turned up her nose at Laura and her friends. Whenever they asked her to go walking with them during recess, Nellie always said no. She said she didn't want to spoil her complexion. And she was always complaining that everything about the town was too rough.

Even with Nellie Oleson in town, Laura liked living in De Smet. When her chores were finished and her homework done, there were always new things to do and people to see.

One Saturday afternoon, Mary Power came to Pa's store to see Laura. Her cheeks were pink with excitement. There was going to be a dime sociable next Friday night. It was going to be in Mrs.

Tinkham's rooms over the furniture store. Everyone was invited.

"I'll go if you do, Laura," Mary Power said. She turned to Ma and asked, "Oh, please may she go, Mrs. Ingalls?"

Ma said that Laura could go to the sociable.

Laura did not know what a dime sociable was, but she didn't want to ask Mary. She liked Mary so much, but she always felt a little shy around her. Mary Power's father was the town tailor. Her clothes were always so beautiful because her father made them.

And Mary always wore her hair in the stylish new way, with bangs. Her hairstyle was called the "lunatic fringe."

All the next week, Laura and Mary Power talked about the sociable. It cost a dime, so Minnie and Ida couldn't go.

Nellie turned up her nose and said she didn't want to go.

Friday seemed long to Laura and Mary. They were so ready for night to come.

That night Laura did not take off her pretty school dress. She put on a long apron and helped with supper. As soon as she had washed the dishes, she began to get ready for the sociable.

Ma helped her carefully brush her dress. It was a very grown-up dress, made from brown wool. It had brown buttons and red around the wrists and collar. The collar was high, and the skirt came just to the tops of Laura's high-buttoned shoes.

Laura stood in front of the mirror. She carefully braided her long brown hair and pinned it up. Then she took it down. She looked in the mirror and tried again. But she could not make her hair look the way she wanted it to.

Finally, she turned to Ma, and asked in a pleading voice, "Oh, Ma, I do wish you would let me cut bangs. Mary Power wears them, and they are so stylish."

"Your hair looks nice the way it is," said Ma. "Mary Power is a nice girl, but I understand why the new hairstyle is called a 'lunatic fringe.'"

"Your hair looks beautiful, Laura," Carrie said to Laura. "It's such a pretty brown and so long and thick. It shines in the light."

Laura still gazed unhappily at the mirror. She looked carefully at the short hairs that grew around her forehead. They did not show when they were brushed back, so she combed them out and down. They made a thin little fringe.

"Oh, please, Ma," Laura coaxed. "I

wouldn't cut heavy bangs, like Mary Power's. Please let me cut just a little more, so I can curl it across my forehead."

At last, Ma gave in. "Very well," she said.

Laura took the scissors from Ma's workbasket. She stood before the glass. She carefully cut the hair above her forehead into a fringe about two inches long.

Then she laid her long slate pencil on the heater. When it was heated, she held it by the cool end and wound wisps of hair around the heated end. Holding each wisp tightly around the pencil, she curled all the bangs.

She combed the rest of her hair smoothly back and braided it. She wound the long braid around on the back of her head. Then she snugly pinned it.

"Turn around and let me see you," Ma said when Laura was finished.

Laura turned and smiled at Ma.

"Do you like it?" she asked.

"It looks quite nice," Ma admitted.

"Turn this way and let me see," said Pa. He looked at her a long minute, and his eyes were pleased. "Well, if you must wear this 'lunatic fringe,' I think you've made a good job of it."

"I think it is pretty. You look very nice," Carrie said softly.

Laura put on her brown coat. She carefully pulled on her brown woolen hood that was lined with blue.

She took one more look in the glass. Her cheeks were pink with excitement. The curled bangs were stylish under the hood, and the blue lining made her eyes very blue.

Ma gave her a dime and said, "Have a good time, Laura. I am sure you'll remember your manners."

"Should I go with her as far as the door, Caroline?" Pa asked.

"It's early yet, and only across the street," Ma answered. "And she's going with Mary Power."

Laura went out into the dark night. The sky was full of stars. Her heart was beating fast. She was going to her very first sociable.

CHAPTER 6

The Sociable

Together, Laura and Mary Power climbed the stairs above the furniture store. They were both quiet. Laura could tell that Mary was as nervous as she was.

Mary Power knocked on the door, and Mrs. Tinkham opened it. Mrs. Tinkham was a tiny woman in a black dress with white lace ruffles. She said good evening, and took Mary's dime and Laura's.

Then she said, "Come this way to leave your wraps."

All week Laura had wondered what a

sociable was. Now she was here. She looked around the room. Some people were sitting in chairs.

Laura felt shy as she followed Mrs. Tinkham past everyone into a small bedroom. She and Mary Power laid their coats and hoods on the bed. Then quietly they slipped into chairs in the larger room.

The room was very handsome. There was a bright flowered carpet covering the whole floor. The glass windows had curtains. A large glass lamp sat on a polished table. The lamp had a white china shade with pretty red roses painted all over it. And there were pictures on the walls with heavy gold frames.

Mr. and Mrs. Woodworth were sitting on a sofa. Cap Garland's older sister, Florence, was there, with their mother. Other ladies from town sat in the nice

chairs around the room. They were all dressed up and silent.

Mary Power and Laura did not speak either. They did not know what to say.

Someone knocked at the door. Mrs. Tinkham hurried to it, and Reverend and Mrs. Brown came in. Reverend Brown's deep voice filled the room with greetings to everyone. Then he talked with Mrs. Tinkham about the home he had left in Massachusetts.

"Not much like this place," he said. "But we are all strangers here."

Laura did not think she liked Reverend Brown. His face was large and bony. His eyes were sunk deep under shaggy white eyebrows and they shone hot and fierce even when he was smiling. His coat hung loose on his big body. And his hands at the end of the sleeves were large and rough with big knuckles.

He talked a great deal. After he came, the others talked some, except Mary Power and Laura. They tried to sit politely, but now and then they fidgeted.

It was a long time before Mrs. Tinkham began to bring plates from the kitchen. On each plate was a small dish of custard and a piece of cake.

When Laura had eaten hers, she whispered to Mary, "Let's go home."

Mary answered, "Come on, I'm going."

They set their empty dishes on a small table near them. They put on their coats and hoods and said good-bye to Mrs. Tinkham.

As soon as they were outside on the street, Laura drew a deep breath.

"Whew!" she said, "if that is a sociable, then I don't like sociables."

"Neither do I," Mary Power agreed. "I wish I hadn't gone. I'd rather have the dime!"

Pa and Ma looked up in surprise when Laura came in.

"Did you have a good time, Laura?" Carrie asked eagerly.

"Well, no, I didn't," Laura had to admit. "You should have gone, Ma, instead of me. Mary Power and I were the only girls there. We had no one to talk to."

"This is only the first sociable in town," Ma said. "When folks here get to know each other better, the sociables will be more interesting."

Laura nodded her head to be polite, but inside she wasn't so sure. She didn't think she wanted to go to a sociable again.

CHAPTER 7

A Birthday Party

A few weeks later, the family was sitting by the fire after supper, when a knock sounded at the door. An envelope had arrived. It was addressed to Miss Laura Ingalls, De Smet, Dakota Territory.

Laura opened the letter and read it out loud.

Ben M. Woodworth
requests the pleasure of
your company at his home
Saturday Evening
January 28th
Supper at Eight o'clock

58

Laura was so surprised, she sat down in a chair and stared at the letter. Ma took it from her hand, and read it again.

"It's a party," Ma said. "A supper party."

"Oh, Laura! You're asked to a party!" Carrie exclaimed.

For a whole week, Laura could not think about anything but the party. She wanted to go, and she did not want to go. She was excited and scared at the same time.

At school everyone was looking forward to the party. Arthur had told Minnie that it would be a birthday party, for Ben's birthday. But the boys and girls could not talk about it at recess and at noon break, because Nellie had not been invited. She could not have come because she lived in the country.

On the night of the party, Laura was dressed and ready at seven o'clock. Mary Power was coming to walk with her to Ben's house.

Laura could not sit still while she waited for Mary. She stood up to take one more look at the mirror on the wall.

She was wearing her Sunday-best dress. It was blue and had little green buttons that went up the front. The skirt was long and full. It had a band of blue and gold and green plaid that went all the way around the skirt, just above the hem. The little collar had a frill of white lace inside it.

Laura had braided her hair and coiled it so that the thick braid covered the back of her head. Her little bangs curled nicely over her forehead.

Laura turned from the mirror and went

to the window. Mary Power was nowhere in sight. Suddenly, Laura was so afraid of the party, she was sure she simply could not go. She wondered if the party was going to be as unpleasant as the sociable had been.

"Sit down and wait quietly, Laura," Ma said gently.

Just then, Laura saw Mary Power. Quickly, she pulled on her coat and her hood, and rushed outside.

When Laura and Mary reached Ben's house, they stood outside and wondered what to do. The upstairs windows were brightly lighted. A lamp burned in the office downstairs, where Ben's older brother, Jim, was working. Jim operated the electric telegraph, a machine that sent messages to far away places.

Mary Power asked Laura, "Do we

knock, or should we just go right in?"

"I don't know," Laura said. She felt better knowing that Mary was not sure, too.

Mary Power waited. Then she knocked. She did not knock loudly, but the sound made them both jump.

No one came. Bravely, Laura said, "Let's go right in!"

She took hold of the door handle, then suddenly Ben opened the door.

"Good evening," Ben said. He was wearing his Sunday suit with a white collar. His hair was damp and carefully combed.

Laura and Mary followed Ben silently. At the top of the stairs, Ben's mother was waiting for them. She wore a soft gray dress with snowy white ruffles at her throat and wrists. She was plump and friendly, and Laura felt better right away.

Mrs. Woodworth told them to take off their coats and go into the sitting room. Ida and Minnie, Arthur and Cap, and Ben were already there.

The sitting room was warm and cozy. There were pretty, shaded lamps and dark red curtains at the windows. The chairs were placed around the stove. The coals glowed red through the stove's glass door.

When Laura looked around she saw a photograph album sitting on a table with a marble top. There were other books nearby. Laura wanted to sit quietly and look at those books, but she knew it would be rude not to talk to the others.

As soon as all the boys and girls were settled in their seats, everyone was quiet. No one said a word.

Laura knew she should say something, but she couldn't think of anything to say. She looked down at her feet. They seemed much too big. She did not know what to do with her hands.

Laura glanced at the other girls. None of them knew what to say, either. Laura's heart sank. She wondered if parties were always this uncomfortable.

Suddenly, they heard the sound of footsteps springing up the stairs. Ben's brother, Jim, came bursting into the room. He looked around at them all sitting so quietly, and he started to laugh.

Then they all started to laugh, too. After that they were able to talk.

When supper was ready, Mrs. Woodworth called them into the dining room.

The room was beautiful. China and silver sparkled across a crisp white table-cloth. A glass lamp hung from the ceiling on golden chains.

At the long table, there were eight plates. The plates were white china with tiny flowers around the edges. Beside each plate was a stiff white napkin.

But best of all, there was an orange in front of each plate. The orange had been cut to look like a flower. Its red-gold petals curled away from the center of the orange. Laura's mouth watered just looking at it.

Mrs. Woodworth told them all where to sit. Now Laura's feet were under the table, and her hands had something to do.

The food was delicious. There was steaming hot soup with tiny crackers. There were stacks of crispy golden brown potato patties. And there were piping hot biscuits with fresh, yellow butter.

After all that, there was a white-frosted birthday cake. Mrs. Woodworth set the cake down in front of Ben so he could cut it.

Carefully, Ben put one slice on each plate, and Mrs. Woodworth handed the plates around. They all waited until Ben had cut his own slice of cake.

As Laura waited, she wondered about the orange in front of her. She didn't know if they were supposed to eat it or not. She had eaten only part of an orange once before. She couldn't imagine having a whole orange to herself.

Everyone took a bite of cake, but no one touched their orange. Laura thought that maybe they were supposed to take their oranges home. Then she could share it with Pa and Ma, and Carrie and Grace.

Just then, Ben picked up his orange. He held it carefully over his plate. He broke the orange into its sections. He took a bite from one section, then he took a bite of cake.

Laura reached for her orange, and so did everyone else. They all divided their oranges into sections just as Ben had done.

Laura took a bite of orange and then a bite of cake. The sweet cake and the tangy orange tasted so good together.

When she was finished eating, Laura

remembered to wipe her lips with her napkin and fold it, just like Ma had told her to do.

"Now we'll go downstairs and play games," Ben said.

The big room downstairs was bright and cheery with light from the wall lamps. It was warm and cozy from the red-hot stove. And there was plenty of room to play the liveliest of games.

They played drop the handkerchief, and then blindman's buff. They played until they were out of breath. Finally, they all dropped panting onto the benches to rest.

"I know a game you've never played!" Jim said after a little while.

They all wanted to know what it was.

"Well, I don't believe it's got a name, it's so new," Jim answered. "But you all come into my office and I'll show you how it's played."

They all crowded into Jim's small office. Jim told them to stand in a half circle and join hands.

"Now stand still," he told them.

They all stood perfectly still, wondering what would happen next.

Suddenly, a burning tingle flashed through Laura. All the clasped hands jerked. The girls screamed, and the boys yelled. Laura was so startled she made no sound and did not move.

Everyone, except for Laura, cried out at once, "What was that? What was it? What did you do, Jim? Jim how did you do that?"

Cap said, "I know it was your electricity, Jim, but how did you do it?"

Jim only laughed and looked at Laura.

"Didn't you feel anything?" he asked her.

"Oh, yes! I felt it," Laura answered.

"Then why didn't you yell?" Jim wanted to know.

Laura wasn't sure why she had stayed quiet. She had been too surprised to call out.

"What was it?" she asked Jim now.

But Jim could only answer, "Nobody knows."

They were all quiet, looking at Jim's telegraph machine. Laura remembered what Pa had told her about electricity. Nobody knew what it was exactly. Benjamin Franklin had discovered that it was lightning, but nobody really knew what lightning was, either. Now electricity worked the electric telegraph, and still nobody knew what it was.

Just then Jim made one click on the telegraph machine, and Laura knew the machine was sending that click far and fast away.

"That's heard in St. Paul," Jim told them.

"Right now?" Minnie asked.

"Right now," Jim nodded.

They were still standing silent around the machine when Pa opened the door and walked in.

"Is the party over?" he asked with a smile. "I've come to see my girl home."

The big clock was striking ten. They were all surprised. No one had noticed how late it was. And no one wanted the party to end.

The boys put on their coats and caps and the girls went upstairs to thank Mrs. Woodworth. Laura buttoned up her coat and tied on her hood.

"Oh! What a good time we had!" Laura and Minnie and Mary all cried at once.

When Laura and Pa got home, Ma was waiting up. Carrie and Grace were already asleep.

"I can see you had a good time because your eyes are shining," Ma said. "Now slip quietly up to bed. Tomorrow you can tell us all about the party."

Laura started upstairs.

"Oh, Ma," Laura couldn't help saying then, "each one of us had a whole orange!"

But she saved the rest to tell them all together.

Now that the party was over, Laura wished it had lasted longer. She would never again be afraid to go to a party. Laura knew that parties were always fun when good friends were there.